I GO QUIET

For Gabrielle

For information about permission to reproduce selections from this book, write to
Permissions, W. W. Norton & Company, Inc., 500 Fifth Avenue, New York, NY 10110

For information about special discounts for bulk purchases, please contact
W. W. Norton Special Sales at specialsales@wwnorton.com or 800-233-4830

Library of Congress Catoaloging-in-Publication Data

Names: Ouimet, David, author, illustrator.
Title: I go quiet / David Ouimet.
Description: First American edition. | New York : Norton Young Readers, [2020] | Audience: Ages 6-9.
Identifiers: LCCN 2019032138 | ISBN 9781324004431 (hardcover) | ISBN 9781324004448 (epub)
Subjects: CYAC: Quietude—Fiction. | Loneliness—Fiction. | Books and reading—Fiction.
Classification: LCC PZ7.1.O884 Iag 2020 | DDC [E]—dc23
LC record available at https://lccn.loc.gov/2019032138

W. W. Norton & Company, Inc., 500 Fifth Avenue, New York, N.Y. 10110
www.wwnorton.com

W. W. Norton & Company Ltd., 15 Carlisle Street, London W1D 3BS

1 2 3 4 5 6 7 8 9 0

I GO QUIET

DAVID OUIMET

NORTON YOUNG READERS

An Imprint of W. W. Norton & Company
Independent Publishers Since 1923

Sometimes, I go quiet.

When I speak
I'm not understood.
So I go quiet.

When I walk into a room,
I hear whispers,

I don't know how I am supposed to be.
I am timid. I am small.
How should I sound?
How should I look?
When it's my turn
to speak,
I go
quiet.

Sometimes I feel
like a rock in a rattle;
yet I make no sound.

I am different.
I am the note
that's not in tune.
I go mousy. I go gray.

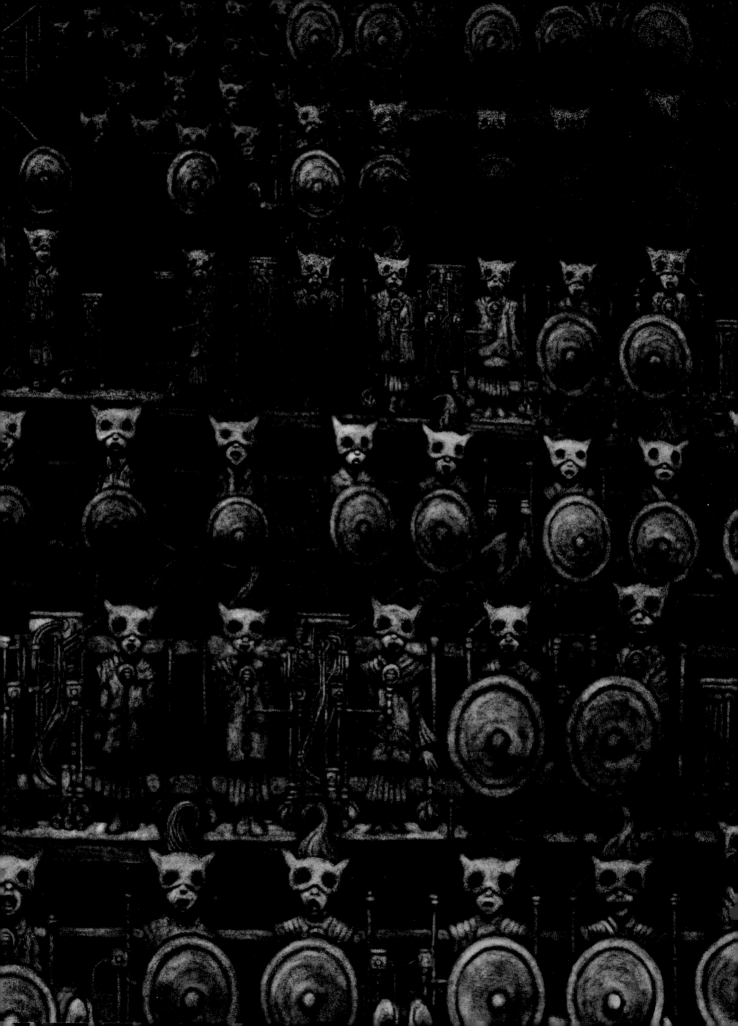

Sometimes
I move
away
from
other
voices.

I sing silence as loud as I can.

I sink into
a slow-moving
smog.

I don't always listen.
My thoughts wander to other things.

I would leave if I could fly.

From time to time I imagine
where I'd like to be.

I shed
my black velvet cape
and I soar,
like a shiny raven.

Sometimes when I go quiet I read.

When I read, I know there are languages that I will speak.

When I read,
I know there is
a world beneath
my branches.

When I read, I feel that every
living thing is part of me.

I think I may be part of everything too.

I am not so different.

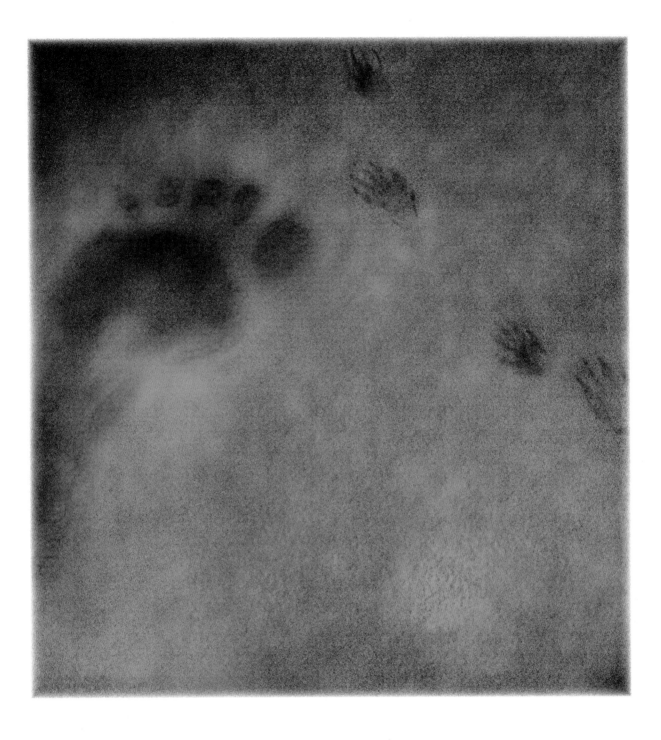

And I am not small.

When I am heard

I will build cities
with my words

They will not be quiet.

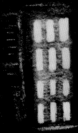

Yes, sometimes I go quiet.

But someday I will make
a shimmering
noise.